THE ADV

Harvey
and Lucy

THE MARSHLAND RESCUE

First published in the UK in 2020
by Little Steps Publishing
Uncommon, 126 New King's Rd, London SW6 4LZ
www.littlestepspublishing.co.uk
ISBN: 978-1-912678-21-1
Text copyright © 2020 Maria Atlan
Illustration copyright © 2020 Adriana Santos

A CIP catalogue record for this book is available from the British
Library.
Designed by Celeste Hulme
Printed in China
10 9 8 7 6 5 4 3 2 1

THE ADVENTURES OF

Harley and Lucy

THE MARSHLAND RESCUE

MARIA ATLAN

Little Steps PUBLISHING

"In a field of horses be a unicorn"
This book is dedicated in loving memory to
Mamie Brisker Pettit
And to all my beautiful animal loving unicorns of
Boquete, Panama whom I love so dearly.

CONTENTS

1
THE MEETING

Harley nervously paced the floor, back and forth, forth and back, muttering orders to himself under his breath. Good posture, Harley. Strong paw shake. The first impression is the most important one so make it count, old boy.

You see, Harley had a good reason for being nervous … well, a few of them, actually. Today was Harley's first day as a retired military service dog and he was being introduced to his new family, Mamie and Greg Lacey, for the first time.

All that pacing came to a stop, however, the moment Sergeant Garcia, Harley's handler and battle buddy, called him into position.

Years of honourable and distinguished service had taught Harley to swallow any feelings of nervousness or anxiety, and to appear calm even in the face of the storm. He was as disciplined and battle tested as any canine could ever hope to be.

So why all the mental fuss? Why the nerves? he kept wondering to himself. *Aren't I supposed to be looking forward to retirement, lying poolside in a sunny backyard, instead of humping it up a steep Central Asian mountain in freezing weather? Eating fancy schmancy savoury nuggets of meat instead of the standard military-issue kibble?* (Which, it turns out, was tough enough to be used as a weapon, as he had once unexpectedly found out during a surprise night raid.)

Could it be because he was going to miss Sergeant Garcia, his best friend and long-time companion? They had both known this day would come. Sergeant Garcia was being deployed on another tour, and the time had come for Harley to close the active-duty chapter of his life and start another.

Perhaps Harley was afraid of change itself, afraid of taking a step into the unknown and unfamiliar. It is a life experience we have all had, and one that many of us dread. Harley, however, was not ready to ask himself if he was afraid, or to think about what it might mean if he answered that question honestly. So, instead, he focused on the one thing he knew to be true and that he could at the moment deal with: that he was going to miss Sergeant Garcia.

Harley was looking straight ahead, sitting tall and alert, when the Laceys walked into the meeting room. Mamie Lacey, a tall woman with a sweet smile and soft brown wavy hair that had little streaks of sunshine in it, let out a squeal of pure delight and immediately dropped down to one knee to pet our stoic Harley.

'Oh, my! What a handsome boy you are. Greg darling, look how handsome he is!' Mamie proclaimed.

Harley's insides warmed to the tenderness in her voice and his posture relaxed at the softness of her touch.

While the Laceys and Sergeant Garcia chitchatted and exchanged stories, Harley began to excitedly wonder about his new life and what could be waiting for him. Mamie seems so nice … and she gives an amazing behind-the-ear scratch … what dog couldn't get used to that! he thought. And Greg is a former military man himself—he seems like a pretty respectable fellow.

Harley wondered if there were going to be any other dogs in the household. Well, no worries there if that's the case, he thought. Old Harley knows how to take charge. I'll have those pups whipped into shape in no time.

Yes, the idea of training and leading a new platoon of canines was so pleasing to him that he soon found himself lost in thought and daydreaming about the possibilities. So it caught him by surprise when Sergeant Garcia kneeled before him with moist eyes and a single tear rolling down his square jaw.

'Well, old boy, it's been a long and sometimes crazy road we've travelled together,' he said. 'But we did it together and I would not have it any other way. Stay strong, stay true and always be brave because even if you can't see me, I am with you and you'll be with me in my thoughts and in my heart. May this next adventure be your greatest one. I love you, Harley.'

And, with what turned into a very wet goodbye hug, followed by a proper salute to his furry brother-in-arms, Sergeant Garcia turned and walked away.

The Laceys could not have been more

kind and understanding. They gave Harley the time and support (via nuzzles and soft head strokes) that he needed to compose himself and mentally prepare for the upcoming trip to his new home.

Harley's sadness subsided, but not because he had quickly forgotten Sergeant Garcia. Harley understood that missing someone can be a good and positive thing. It means that person brought happiness into your life, and they now occupy a place in your heart that can never be taken away, even when they're gone.

Harley thought about all of this and repeated Sergeant Garcia's words to himself: Be strong, be true, be brave. All right, old boy, he thought, it's time to pull yourself up by the doggy bootstraps and start this new chapter.

And that is exactly what Harley did.

With head held high and optimism shining from every hair on his beautiful coat, Harley walked down the footpath side by side with the Laceys, got into the family car and drove off towards his new life. Everything was going great ... until the door of his new life and home were opened.

Before him was not the solitude of a single-pet home, not even the platoon of ragtag pups he had hoped to lead, but a tiny, bushy-tailed, tri-coloured cat.

A fudgen C.A.T.!

Harley had unknowingly been taken to a feline encampment. He now found himself behind enemy lines.

2
LUCY GETS A BROTHER

Lucy watched from her cosy living-room perch with a mixture of excitement and curiosity as the Laceys pulled into their driveway. She was getting a new brother and she could not be happier. The whole week had been filled with anticipation and excitement that only grew as 'The Day' (as it became known in the Lacey household) neared. Now it was finally here.

Gracefully propping herself up into a

sitting position in order to have a better view of her new sibling, Lucy thought how composed and stoic he seemed, as well as handsome (well, for a dog, anyway). As soon as she heard the keys jingling in the front door, she jumped off her sun-warmed ledge and sauntered (in the way only cats can) to the front door. Lucy wanted to greet her family and give their new member a proper and warm welcome.

The words 'Lucy, this is Har–' had barely managed to leave Greg Lacey's lips before Lucy was affectionately purring and rubbing her soft flank around Harley, who was seated completely upright. You see, in cat culture this is a sign of acceptance and a way of expressing a sort of personal claim. By rubbing her scent onto his, Lucy was saying to the world: This is my dog, my brother, my family.

As Lucy continued to figure-eight around Harley, she could feel him stiffening and drawing into himself. Lucy, however, was not offended. This was due to the fact that while Lucy was indeed a young cat she was also a very wise one. The lessons and experiences in her life had taught her much, and what is universally true of all wise creatures, whether they are people like you, or cats, or dogs or even alligators, is that they all perceive and consequently react to the world around them with understanding and compassion.

Lucy understood that Harley was most likely nervous. Being new to any situation can create insecurities and fears in even the most confident and brave among us.

So Lucy resolved to accept, be patient

with and love Harley just as he was. Eventually he would grow accustomed to his new home, family and life. Lucy knew that when this happened, Harley's walls would begin to come down, and he would let her into his heart as well.

My dear reader, this is an important lesson in life: fear and insecurity often create walls and divisions, some bigger and deeper than others. This happens in all communities. However, understanding, patience and sincere love through compassion can bring down walls, bridge divisions and create beautiful consequences like friendship, happy and supportive communities, and ultimately a kinder world. Never forget that a smile, a kind hello or even a small show of understanding can change the entire course of someone's day, adding a bright light in what might have been darkness. Kindness can be as contagious as chickenpox; it spreads from one person to another, extending out to people you haven't even met.

After feeling satisfied that she had given Harley a proper hello, Lucy gracefully stepped back and gave Harley some space to check out his new surroundings. After he'd done a bit of exploring, the Laceys brought Harley into the kitchen for dinner (something which he got quite excited about).

Lucy chuckled to herself as Harley energetically followed the Laceys. She knew that tonight the Laceys would be preoccupied with Harley and getting him acquainted with his new home. She also knew Harley was in good and loving hands, so she took the opportunity to head out a little early, via her cat door in the garage, to her monthly Cat Community meeting.

3
AN EVENTFUL BREAKFAST

As the soft glow of morning's first light stretched across the world and began to creep into the Laceys' home, it brought with it a brand-new day – a day filled with new possibilities and adventures. Harley stretched lazily from his comfortable bed and looked over at his new humans, who were also beginning to wake.

Well, adventures can wait, Harley thought.

First, breakfast and a good tummy rub are in order.

Harley had spent a relaxing and lovely evening with the Laceys while getting to know his new home. They made him feel welcomed, wanted and loved. This helped to alleviate some of his anxiety about going through such a major life change. The cat Lucy, however, had put him on edge. Harley didn't know if her show of affection the previous night had been about ownership or about proclaiming territorial rights, a message of 'This is my home' or 'These are my humans'. But he figured that whatever the intended message was, it couldn't be a good one.

He decided he would have to keep an eye on Lucy; he had learned from his military experience that it was always better to be prepared to face the enemy then to be taken by surprise. However, the truth was that Harley didn't know many cats and the little contact he had experienced usually resulted in them running away from him … not walking right up to him and rubbing his fur.

Yes, this one is a bold one, Harley thought. *She doesn't seem to fear me. I had better be on alert around her.*

Before he could give the matter any more thought, Mamie Lacey's voice cut through the mental minefield he was getting lost in by sweetly asking, 'Does my handsome boy want to go for a walk and have some brekkie?'

She calls breakfast 'brekkie'! That's so cute, Harley thought, smiling to himself.

So up they got and went on a much-needed morning walk, which was followed by a delicious bowl of dog chow for Harley and an always-appreciated tummy rub from Mamie Lacey. Ahhh, this is the life, Harley thought happily as he relaxed next to Greg Lacey, who (much to Harley's delight) fed him bites of sausage when Mamie Lacey wasn't looking.

As the Laceys continued to eat their breakfast and read the newspaper, Harley began to drift off into a sausage-induced sleep … until Lucy walked into the room.

Harley realised that he hadn't seen her since their initial introduction the night before. This morning she seemed somewhat different – not the peppy and bubbly cat he had met the night before, but tense and lost in thought. That, however, immediately changed the moment Mamie called out to Lucy. After giving a sweet meow, Lucy jumped onto Mamie's lap for a snuggle.

'Darling, listen to this.' Greg was reading a story in the newspaper. 'Developers are putting in a bid with the City Chamber of Commerce to tear down Old Ashley Place. They want to build a housing development.'

Mamie Lacey turned to look at her husband with a very startled and upset look upon her face. 'What about the marsh, and all the animals that call it home?' she said. 'I thought the area was protected! And what about the Old Ashley farmhouse? It has so much history. It shouldn't be torn down at the expense of the environment and our local history, just so people can have an apartment overlooking the harbour!'

Mamie rarely got this agitated about a situation, so Greg replied with empathy. 'No, of course not, dear,' he said. 'You're right, of course. Something should be done to protect the marsh and Old Ashley Place.'

As the wheels of thought began to turn in her head, Mamie's look changed from angry to determined. She was beginning to form a plan.

But what had caught Harley's eye was Lucy's reaction to the Laceys' discussion. She again seemed as tense as she had when she'd first walked into the room. Harley couldn't help wondering what it was all about. He had felt the mood of the room change. But it would be much later that he realised the shift was the same one he'd always felt before he embarked on an important mission.

4
LUCY'S PAST

Lucy listened attentively while the Laceys discussed the newspaper article detailing the marshland development project. The same situation had been discussed the night before during the Cat Community meeting. The group was trying to form an action plan in case the housing development apartment project was given the green light by the City Chamber of Commerce, which would threaten the lives and homes of all the unique and wonderful creatures that called the marshland their home.

And while saving the marshland and its inhabitants was very important to Lucy, she was particularly worried about three inhabitants of Old Ashley Place: her aunts. These three lovely felines were not biologically her kin, but they were her family. This happens when the bonds of love are so strong that they bring together and create families, even when we don't share a bloodline.

Worrying about her aunts and the possible destruction of their home, Lucy began to think about the day she had met them and how they had helped to shape her life.

You see, when Lucy was a kitten, she

was adopted by a very large family with lots of children. This meant the house was always filled with lots of noise and a little bit of chaos. One day, shortly after she was adopted, the family's father found better employment in another town, and so they had to move. Amid the packing, confusion and overall stress that accompanies moving, Lucy was left behind.

Now we will go ahead and assume that this was by accident, because otherwise the act of deliberately leaving a kitten behind is far too cruel for me (and for you, my dear reader, I am sure) to imagine. However, whether it was by accident or on purpose, Lucy was a wise cat, so she believed in forgiveness. Because to hold a grudge only hurts the grudge-holder, and Lucy had far too much sparkle to let anyone dull her shine. This lesson was one she learned in time and through the loving mentoring of her three aunts.

Lucy waited around the house for a few days but when the food supply began to dwindle, she decided she would go out and look for her missing family. Being only a kitten and having never ventured out very far on her own, Lucy quickly got lost among the giant oak trees and thick brush that surrounded the marsh. Scared and disoriented, she found shelter in the overgrown roots of a willow tree, where she lay down and began to sing softly to herself in an attempt to feel less lonely. She was well into the chorus of her second song when the stalks of the reeds surrounding the willow tree began to sway and bend, forming a grassy passageway from which emerged a large, elegant silver Persian cat walking gracefully towards her.

'What are you doing out here alone in the marsh, little one? Are you lost?' she gently asked Lucy. 'This can be a dangerous place for those unfamiliar with its hazards. Are you hungry?'

Lucy shyly nodded her head.

'Better come with me. I'll take you to a warm, dry place where you can fill your belly with yummy food, and rest safely while you tell me how you got out here all by yourself.'

Feeling the first rays of hope enter her heart since she had been left behind, Lucy jumped up and followed the kind silver cat through the reeds and thick brush.

'Thank you for helping me. I am called Lucy.'

'Well it's very nice to meet you Lucy,' the silver cat replied. 'I am Fiona and, when we get to my home you'll also get to meet my sisters Susan and Diana. They might seem a little eccentric at first but they're really quite lovely. Exceptional and beautifully unique personalities are often called "odd" or "strange", but this is mostly due to ignorance, or a lack of imagination or understanding. However, the beautiful thing about ignorance is that it is not a permanent state of existence. With education and patience it can be remedied, and the once-ignorant individual can go on to live a very enlightened and colourful life—in rainbow colours, instead of one that is all khaki,' Fiona explained with a smile.

Through a maze of low-hanging limbs

of ancient trees, and thick, seemingly endless grass banks that cut in and out of snaking waterways, Lucy followed Fiona. They continued until finally the forest gave way to a glade. In the centre of the clearing, overlooking the soft-lapping waves of the harbour, was an old but charming farmhouse.

'Well, we're home, sweet pea. Come inside and meet the girls. We don't often have such lovely and delightful company over for dinner. They'll both be very excited to meet you.'

And with the opening and closing of the farmhouse front door, Lucy entered a new chapter in her life, one that would be filled with love, affection and thoughtfulness. In time, Fiona, Susan and Diana would be transformed from kind strangers into

Lucy's family: her much-beloved aunts.

You see, there is a wonderful and very important lesson here, and that is to never give up. No matter how bleak things may seem, life can always surprise you and turn around. Who knows what magnificent adventures and experiences await you in the unwritten chapters of your life? Today you might feel sad and wounded, but happiness and healing may be just around the corner.

Remembering that day, Lucy sighed sadly. Although it was a beautiful memory, she could not separate it from the anxiety and fear she felt knowing her family could be in danger. Her aunts, who had given her a home when she most needed it, now faced the possibility of losing theirs.

The very thought of it fuelled Lucy's

resolve. She would go to them as soon as possible and rescue them. After all, it had been her aunts who had taught her that action is required if you want to make a difference and help make the world a better place.

5
THE TOWN MEETING

Deep in thought, Mamie Lacey slowly walked up the stone steps of the town's city hall. She knew the facts of her argument, but she wanted to ensure that she conveyed the importance of her message to the townspeople. She needed them to open their eyes, minds and hearts to the necessity of protecting the marshland.

Stopping just outside the entrance to the city hall, Mamie Lacey leaned back on the verandah and reverently looked over the beautiful colonial building. Built at the turn of the nineteenth century, the once bright-salmon–coloured paint had now faded to a light pink; ivy and mould crept upwards on elegant columns. This was a place of history and strength and it was that very feeling Mamie hoped she would be able to capture and express at the meeting.

Mamie Lacey nervously made her way up the aisle, politely nodding and smiling at the many familiar faces beginning to fill the auditorium. Seated in a half-circle on the raised platform at the front of the room were the town leaders, and several representatives of Coastal Networks Management Inc. (ConMan), the developers who wanted to destroy the marsh in order to build on it. She couldn't help but observe the smug looks on their faces and secretly hoped she would somehow be able to wipe them off.

Moments later the town council leader called for everyone to take their seats, and with that the meeting began.

ConMan's representatives presented their project to the town, using a very well-put-together slide show showcasing what the new development would look like. Their speeches and images were both enticing and persuasive. Mamie could see how easy it would be for someone to be lured in by the intelligent marketing scheme, and just how much more difficult it would make it for her to convince her community that they couldn't let ConMan continue with the project. However, Mamie was not a woman easily deterred, especially now that she knew the entire marshland environmental community was depending on her.

When the presentation was finished, Mamie Lacey took a deep breath, stood up and asked for the microphone.

'Hi everyone, I am Mamie Lacey,' she began, 'and I am here today to speak on behalf of those who cannot stand here and speak for themselves. I am talking about the marshland and all the inhabitants that call the marsh home.

'I understand how alluring ConMan's proposition is, with its new modern housing, golf courses that look fun and are well designed, and the amenities – especially the resort-style pools – are particularly inviting. But I ask you: at what price? What is the price that must be paid for this dream they are selling?

'The price is the destruction and loss of our community's unique and precious natural habitat. The price is the demolition of Old Ashley Place, a place of history and regional pride. The price is the devastation of hundreds if not thousands of plant, land and aquatic species, and completely wiping from the earth some species that are found only in this area. I ask you: is this development worth that price?

'For those of you less concerned about the environment, I ask you: when the annual rains come, as they always do, and the natural sponge-like effect of the marsh that has protected us from flooding for hundreds of years no longer exists, and your homes flood and you lose everything you have worked so hard for, will this development be worth that price?

'I am here not only asking you to stop this project from going forward, but to begin the process to declare the marsh a protected natural environment. We must protect not only the marsh, but our homes as well!'

Much to Mamie Lacey's surprise, claps and cheers began to fill the auditorium as she finished. She released the nervous breath she had been holding. She had reached them.

'Mrs Lacey, is it?' A ConMan representative stood up with an air of confidence. 'That was a very touching and moving speech. However, another price you forgot to include was the price of stopping progress, stopping the jobs that this development could provide and stopping the new money it will bring into your town economy. Are you really trying to prevent your town from obtaining additional jobs and seeing increased cash flow? Are you willing to be the one responsible for halting your town's growth? Why don't we take a vote, and see how your town really feels about rejecting this project.'

Mamie Lacey became uneasy. The man's words had some truth to them, and she feared the town would see it his way. Adding to her uneasiness was the note of arrogant amusement she could hear in his voice.

Feeling irritated by the bold way in which the representative had called for a vote, thus usurping her role, the town council leader stood up and explained the voting process.

She reminded the ConMan visitors that they were there as representatives, not as town administrators.

The vote to stop the project and save the marsh was upheld, although it was fairly close; 65 per cent voted to stop it versus 35 per cent who disagreed. But the marsh would be saved, and Mamie's eyes began to fill with tears of joy and relief. However, before she could express her happiness and gratitude, the ConMan rep stood up again. This time, at a volume everyone could hear, he laughed out loud.

'Ahhh!' he chuckled. 'We thought this might be a possibility. You see, the vote was a mere formality. The permits have already been filed, and so has all the relevant paperwork. Our appeal against this outcome has also already been prepared and will be filed tomorrow.'

The face of the town council leader went ghostly pale. From somewhere in the centre of the room, a shocked town resident cried out. 'I don't understand. What does that mean? We voted in a legal forum against your project. Surely you can't just ignore our decision!'

'Well, actually, we can,' countered the ConMan rep, with that same smug expression on his face. 'According to a new bill, work can begin within 60 days of an appeal filed. The project could be completed before your administrative law court even renders an opinion. You see, opposing us is useless. You might as well get behind us and partake in the benefits this project offers.'

And, just like that, the meeting was over.

The ConMan reps exited the auditorium, leaving a stunned town in their wake.

For a moment Mamie Lacey felt dazed and confused by the turn of events, but the feeling quickly passed as she was overcome with an internal blaze of determination so bright that, if you were an observant person, you would have seen it glowing in her eyes. *This isn't over*, Mamie thought. *We will not accept defeat.*

This determination, my dear reader, is a state of mind that separates those in life who are successful and those who unfortunately are not. In life you will hear the word 'No' many times; you will see doors you thought were open close right in front of you; and you will have to endure loss. But it is those people who do not give up who ultimately succeed. They view a

'No' not as a refusal but as an invitation to find an alternate way. They see a door closed and decide to try another door, or to open a window instead. They take a loss as a lesson on how to improve, and they go back, train harder and try again. There's always more than one way to reach your goal, and Mamie Lacey, who understood and lived by this truth, just had to figure out how to do it.

6
THE ADVENTURE BEGINS

Lucy waited until the Laceys had headed into town and Harley was napping downstairs to make her move. She discreetly made her way up the stairs and out the open bedroom window, dropping onto the rooftop in order to get a bird's-eye view of the town's layout. She needed to find the shortest and cat-friendliest route to get out of town and into the marsh. From the tippy-top of the Lacey home she was able to see which streets would lead her towards the marsh, and which backyards looked like they might have big dogs who would not be too happy to see a cat strolling by.

Having made a mental map of the best route to take, Lucy carefully made her way down the roof and over to the magnolia tree that stood at the side of their home. Nimbly she used the tree's branches to get down and onto the lawn. Lucy looked back at her home for just a moment. She didn't want to worry the Laceys but felt that she didn't have a choice. Her aunts needed her. Taking a deep breath, Lucy began running down the street with long fluid strides, stopping only to hide underneath cars when she spotted someone or something that looked like a potential threat.

After an hour of this street-run/car-dodge tactic, Lucy came to an intersection that had a large blue Victorian house with white trim. This was the marker she was looking for. From her rooftop she had noticed a series of homes, starting with the blue one, that all had seemed to have safe and obstacle-free backyards. Looking both ways and making sure the coast was clear, Lucy bolted across the street, through the blue house's front yard, and, with a leap that would have impressed an Olympic pole-vaulter, into the safety of its backyard.

Now there was more coverage and less commotion than on the open street, she began to feel slightly less tense. Using bushes, trees, fences and any other helpful backyard elements that provided her with climbing and coverage potential, Lucy began making her way through and over one backyard after another. Everything was going smoothly, with only two backyards left in the row, when she heard the deep and unmistakable growl of a large dog.

Looking up, Lucy saw that the source of the menacing sound was running straight for her. Her eyes widened in fear, and panic shot through her like an arrow as she realised her attacker was between her and the escape route. Mustering every ounce of strength she had left, Lucy used the edge of the bench she was standing on as a spring, launching herself over the large ferocious dog a split second before he collided into the bench and into her. The timing was so close that Lucy could feel the wetness of the dog's foamy slobber on her fur. Running faster than she had known was possible, Lucy made it to the yard's only tree and managed to scramble up the trunk and into the safety of its limbs.

Sharp twisted branches scratched her and grabbed at her collar, ripping it off her soft neck as she made her way to the side of the tree that hung over the next yard. With her brain hyperalert and her body full of adrenaline, Lucy nervously surveyed the yard. She did not want to find herself in a similar predicament to the one she had just barely escaped. Once she felt certain of safe passage, Lucy jumped off the tree and quickly made her way out of the neighbourhood.

Feeling uneasy from her close call, Lucy decided to forgo the backyard route she had initially planned for the last section of town. Instead she decided it would be best to go through the long-abandoned industrial zone. It was not only empty but would also lead her out of town and right to the marsh's edge. However, before she even got the chance to take one step towards her newly decided course, Lucy heard the loud shriek of a thrilled little girl, immediately followed by the sensation of two sticky hands grabbing and lifting her into an overexcited bear hug. Hearing the commotion, the little girl's mother ran over to her overjoyed daughter.

'Pumpkin, be careful! You could hurt that sweet kitty if you squeeze her too hard. Here, give her to me,' the little girl's mother gently ordered. 'Let's see if you have a collar,' she said to Lucy. 'I am sure there's a family missing you right about now.'

Remembering that her collar had gotten snagged in the tree during her escape, Lucy let out an irritated and anxious sigh.

'Well, sweet girl, without a collar we don't have a clue who to contact, but you're much too well-kept to be a street cat. So how about I take you with us and we can check with the vet to see if you have a chip, or if anyone has posted flyers looking for you? In the meantime, you can play with my sweet Anna Kate.'

Hearing her mother's last sentence, Anna Kate joyfully jumped up and down, clapping her hands.

Although Anna Kate and her mother seemed like nice people, Lucy didn't want another family. She loved the Laceys. For a brief moment Lucy thought that if she had not lost her collar, at least she would be going back to her home with the Laceys. The thought swiftly passed, however, because Lucy knew that fixating on things you cannot change, like the past, was not only pointless but took away from the time you could be using to come up with a solution to your problem. She was on a mission and would not let this new complication discourage her.

Lucy knew what she had to do, and that was plan her escape.

7
HARLEY MEETS A GATOR

Harley accompanied Mamie Lacey for several hours as they walked up and down the streets of their town hanging up and handing out 'Missing Cat' flyers. Two days ago Harley had watched Lucy walk up the stairs and disappear, not realising that it would be the last time she would be seen. More than 48 hours had passed and the Laceys were in full panic mode. Shelters had been visited, streets scoured, neighbours called … but no one had seen Lucy.

Harley hated to see his new family suffer like this. During the last half hour of their walk he had seriously begun to weigh his options about how best to help. Despite his reservations about this particular feline, Lucy was still part of the family. There was also the possibility that she could be in serious trouble. Harley at his core would always be a brave, loyal and dependable dog of honour, never letting personal feelings get in the way of doing what he knew was right. Besides, he cared about the Laceys and wanted to do everything within his power to help them.

Harley reviewed what he knew about the situation. He recalled that the newspaper article about developing the marsh had upset Lucy. As a matter of fact, it had upset the whole household, in particular Mamie Lacey, who was ping-ponging between worrying about Lucy and finding a way to save the marsh.

There certainly was a possibility that Lucy might be headed there. Along with a million other places, he wearily thought.

After careful consideration of various scenarios, Harley spent the afternoon examining every corner of the house, registering and memorising Lucy's smell, and utilising his highly evolved nose in the hope of tracking her movements. He had proven to be a talented and highly skilled tracker more than once during his military career, even leading a search through heavy jungle to rescue a downed pilot. Having committed Lucy's scent to memory,

Harley decided it would be best to leave at night. This would give him roughly eight hours to look for Lucy without adding any additional worry to the already worried Laceys.

Lying in his bed that night, Harley attentively listened to the Laceys' breathing, waiting for the slow soft inhalations that accompany sleep. (Or loud snores, in some of our cases.) When he was certain they had dozed off, he used his skills in stealth to quietly make his way downstairs ... only to realise he had no idea how to get out of the house. The cat door was far too small for him to fit through, all the doors were locked and the windows were closed.

Not having thought of this basic essential action for his mission, Harley berated himself. Come on, old boy! How can you expect to rescue that cat if you can't even get out of the house?

Looking around, he saw that his only shot of getting outside was ripping through the flimsy mesh screen that enclosed the sunroom. Harley rationalised that as long as he brought Lucy safely home, the Laceys would overlook it. Tucking his chin into his chest so the strong, hard bone of his head would act as a hammer, Harley forcefully bounded through the sunroom, onto the wicker sofa and right through the screen, flying into the cool humid night.

Landing with a thud, he shook off the debris clinging to his coat and immediately put his nose to work. Being that this was also Lucy's yard, it took Harley several minutes to determine which scent was the freshest. Sniffing around the old magnolia tree, Harley used the odour to tell him a story. He now understood that the reason she was last seen going up the stairs was because she had left from the roof and down the tree. Feeling confident he was on the right trail, Harley let Lucy's scent guide him like a map away from the Lacey home.

He ran down streets and through backyards, and stopped once because her scent had slightly changed; he knew from the sudden additional pheromone that she had been afraid here. He made a mental note to come back some other time and have a chat with the dog who he could smell lived here. However, because he could smell that she had continued on, he also kept going. He followed Lucy's scent right to the edge of town, where suddenly it stopped. Not a trace, not even the slightest of clues – her scent just went cold.

Okay, well, what do I do now? Harley wondered. Which way should I go?

Taking stock of where he was, Harley realised that the road he was on led out of town and straight into the marshland. So it must be the newspaper story that was at the root of her disappearance, he reasoned.

Harley knew that the marshland was a complex ecosystem to try to navigate. Filled with maze-like waterways, dense woods and swamps that weaved through its landscape in a dizzying design, it was an easy place for even the most seasoned tracker to get lost in. However, without Lucy's scent to follow, Harley knew this was his only lead. Thinking hard about the conversation that morning, Harley recalled the mention of an old building or house that was in danger of being torn down and replaced with a new housing development. He just couldn't remember the exact name.

Ashton Home? Harley thought, trying to remember. *No. Perhaps Langley Place? That didn't sound quite right either.*

Reasoning that there were probably not many historic buildings in the marsh, Harley decided he would try finding an owl to help him. Why an owl, you ask? Well, owls have a reputation for being wise and dependable and, with their ability to fly, have a fantastic aerial view of the surrounding land and the structures within it.

Continuing past the town limits, Harley left one world and crossed into another. He cautiously moved past the outer rim of trees that framed the marsh's edge, massive storm-tested guardians that he found both impressive and intimidating. Carefully moving over the gnarled, twisted roots that protruded from the forest floor – silent hazards capable of tripping and injuring a careless passer-by – Harley remained alert and listened for the hoot of an owl; however, he only heard the caw of an occasional crow. Having once had a bad experience with a game-playing crow, Harley ignored the caws and continued to travel deeper into the forest.

The darkness soon became so thick and heavy that it enveloped his every sense, and when he heard the gurgle of a nearby creek he let out a deep breath of relief, unaware that until that moment he had been holding it. By following the babble of the flowing water Harley was led to an area where the gaps between the trees began to widen, allowing for pockets of light from the stars and moon to penetrate the blackness. Eventually he came to the opening of a vast glade where the creek smoothly poured itself into one of the marsh's much larger channels. Here Harley could feel the cool breeze on his face as it cut through the saw grass. The sweet smell of night-time flowers filled his nostrils, and all around him he could see the dancing lights of hundreds of fireflies.

Harley instantly loved this space in the world. He found it enchanting. He allowed himself to relax for just a moment and simply enjoy being there.

Feeling renewed and ready to continue in search of Lucy, Harley calmly began to look around him. He was trying to determine which path to take when to his complete shock, followed by immediate terror, he realised he was not alone. There, staring at him from the water's muddy edge and wearing a jagged, razor-sharp toothy grin, was the largest alligator Harley had ever seen.

8
LUCY LEARNS TO WATER SKI

Finding herself driven further and further away from the marsh, Lucy knew she had to act quickly, but the what and the how still eluded her. A few more town blocks went by before the clouds of uncertainty parted: Anna Kate's mother announced they were stopping at the supermarket to pick up groceries for dinner. Lucy knew she had to seize this opportunity as she might not get another.

She began to position herself so she would be able to spring forward off Anna Kate's lap, onto the headrest of the front seat and out the driver's-side door. Lucy was relying on the element of surprise and her own swift actions, hoping that using the headrest would buy her a few additional but necessary moments to bolt out of the car before Anna Kate's mother could react.

Despite the day's earlier scares and setbacks, luck finally appeared to be on Lucy's side. The moment the car engine stopped and Anna Kate's mother opened her door, Lucy put her escape plan into action, successfully launching herself out of the car and into the parking lot. Once again free, Lucy began to run as fast as she could, all the while avoiding moving cars and weaving in and out of the parked ones. Having paid attention to what roads and turns had been taken during her captivity, Lucy quickly made her way to the abandoned industrial area, this time making it to the marsh's edge without any further incidents.

Having grown up there, Lucy was comfortable navigating through the elements and features of the marsh that might confuse and disorient others. Using her memories like friendly signposts, Lucy swiftly made her way past the tangle of roots that carpeted the dense forest. She moved forward towards the channel that would connect her to the sleepy hidden glade on the edge of Old Ashley Place. Here jutting grass mounds and sandbanks rose above the water's surface, forming a natural bridge. The land animals of the swamp used these types of helpful features to connect them to the many estuaries, glades and other areas that would otherwise be isolated in this watery kingdom.

However, when Lucy got to the water's edge, the landscape she had been so familiar with was changed. What lay before her was a sea of softly swaying saw grass, occasionally disrupted by colourful patches of purple and white water lilies. Not a single grass mound or sandbank could be seen.

Lucy thought back to that year's springtime, when the unusually heavy rains had forced her to stay inside for weeks at a time. *Of course, the marsh flooded,* Lucy thought. That much rain would most certainly have caused the water level to swell and swallow up the grass mounds and sandbanks. She remembered being a little miffed about the lack of outdoor play, but had not once thought about how it might affect the marsh or her aunts. She felt a pang of guilt for not thinking past her own immediate world. She was not typically prone to selfishness, but resolved to be more thoughtful of the larger world around her.

Getting back to the matter at hand, Lucy pondered how she might be able to get across the channel and over to the clearing on the other side. Aquatic transportation of some sort would be needed, and she knew just who to ask for help. Using a trick her Aunt Susan had taught her, Lucy immersed her paw in the water and began making figure eights with her claws. After a few minutes, two curious largemouth bass came up to the surface. Bass are known the swamp over as amazing conversationalists; these two remained at the surface, granting Lucy an audience.

Lucy began to explain the situation and the swamp's predicament, and asked if they could as quickly as possible help her locate her friend Nico, the catfish. Nico was one of Lucy's oldest and dearest friends, but he was also a great problem-solver, using creative, out-of-the-box thinking to resolve complex problems that others could not. Much to Lucy's delight (not to her surprise, however, since Nico was quite popular and was often sought when help was needed), the bass knew Nico and in fact had seen him earlier digging a hole in the channel's muddy bottom so that he could burrow into it when the day got hotter. The bass were more than happy to help Lucy, for they were the innately helpful sort and, as a bonus, now had a new story to bring up and discuss in future conversations. They told Lucy to wait right where she was, and they would personally deliver Nico to her.

While Lucy waited, the sun began to dip lower and lower into the sky, painting pink, orange and violet streaks over the marsh. Lucy took this time to think about what she was going to do and say once she was able to reach her aunts. At this point she hadn't given much thought to how she was going to rescue them, instead focusing on her need to reach and physically be with them. However, her thoughts were interrupted by long wiry whiskers followed by a very recognisable broad catfish head breaking through the calm surface of the water, generating circular wakes that made the languid water lilies energetically bob up and down.

'Lucy, my girl!' Nico called out in his deep baritone voice. 'It has been far too long since I last saw you. But from what the bass have told me, we'll have to save our catch-up for another time. It seems we have a marsh and your aunts to save. A most unpleasant surprise indeed! However, to be armed with this information is a far better thing. Knowledge can be a powerful tool; ignorance, however, can only lead to ruin.

'First, we need to get you to Old Ashley Place, then we can all put our heads together and formulate a plan.'

'Oh, Nico, it truly is wonderful to see you, although I wish the situation was different,' Lucy said with a smile of apology – for being the bearer of bad news and for allowing so much time to pass since her last visit.

'No need to worry, my girl. You're here now and that's what counts,' Nico assured her. 'I gave your predicament some thought on my swim here. Typically, Big Dave can help with these types of situations, however he's gone down south to defend another gator's territory claim. Given his absence I've come up with an alternate plan that just might work.

'The bass have gone to round up Wendy Egret and the Turtle boys Owen and Evan. They should be here shortly. While we wait, I need you to use your sharp claws and slice off several pieces of vine hanging from that cypress tree. Make sure to get flexible green ones—the brown ones are brittle and will break when we try to shape them.'

Obediently turning back, Lucy bounded towards the cypress tree and up its rigid trunk. Just as she was cutting off the last needed vine, she heard the distinct beating of great wings getting closer. Wendy and the Turtle boys had arrived.

With all needed participants and supplies gathered around, Nico began to explain his idea. Lucy would wrap two vines around Owen and Evan's shells, inserting her back paws as if into a sandal. The remaining vines would serve as a pulling rope between her and Wendy. Owen and Evan would retract their legs and heads back into their shells for their own comfort and to create a more streamlined shape that would reduce drag and resistance as they were propelled across the water. Once strapped in, Lucy would position her back paws on the back end of Owen and Evan's shells, creating a little lift for greater stability, and using her front paws to grab onto the pulling vine held in Wendy's beak. Maintaining a low flying altitude just above the water, Wendy would pull them (just like a boat pulls a water-skier) across the channel, over the bayou and onto the clearing where Old Ashley Place waited for them.

After several attempts that would have been comical had the situation not been so desperate, two slightly sore turtles, one very wet cat and a remarkably patient egret took off towards the horizon, followed of course by their coach Nico. Thus they successfully formed the hardly-known-about but very impressive world-first multispecies waterskiing team.

9
HARLEY MAKES NEW FRIENDS

Harley knew this was a make-or-break moment. He recalled the gator facts he had learned in predator ambush training. He knew gators were capable of short bursts of speed on land of up to 30 miles per hour. He also knew he didn't stand a chance against this living dinosaur if he got cornered into a water fight. Just as he decided that a zigzag-pattern retreat might be his only option, the massive reptile spoke.

'I say, traveller, I do not wish to offend, but you appear to be lost,' the gator politely stated, in a genteel southern accent. He seemed to have no wish to insult the proud shepherd, and tactfully continued. 'To see a canine such as yourself at this hour, in this part of the swamp, well, let us just say it is an uncommon occurrence. My name is David Allen Esquire, however everyone around these parts just calls me Big Dave.'

While his smooth voice and excellent manners did help Harley feel ever-so-slightly-less terrified, he was still wary of Big Dave and was very much guarded as he completed his half of the introductions.

'Well, Harley, being that I was born and raised here, I know every creek, every channel and every possible waterway. I know where they go and, equally as important, where they do not go. If I might be of any assistance to you, I am here at your disposal.'

While Harley was indeed in desperate need of navigational help, he had his suspicions about Big Dave's offer. After all, he was a lawyer and he also wasn't ready to become anyone's next meal. As Harley contemplated what he should do, his thoughts were interrupted by the sound of a heated conversation getting louder and headed in their direction. One of the group members was clearly worked up and was calling for action now. Soon faces followed voices, and from the low-lying vegetation emerged an agitated raccoon trailed by two sleepy but composed rabbits.

'Dave! There you are, finally! How did the property dispute go?'

Without waiting for an answer, or even taking a breath, the hurried raccoon continued. 'I am not sure if the news made it down south, but we're in serious trouble here – all of us, the whole marsh. Lucy brought the news. She's back and staying with her aunts at Old Ashley Place. I've brought Bella and Michelle with me. We need to get over there, learn the details and formulate a plan as soon as possible. The longer we wait the more we stand to lose; time is of the essence! Ladies, please board first; I'll secure the rear.'

Harley remained momentarily frozen. His ears, his eyes and his long-held viewpoints were experiencing simultaneous shockwaves of disbelief. For his whole canine existence he had thought of raccoons as sneaky, volatile and quite often rabid pests to be avoided. However, this gentleman didn't seem to possess any of those off-putting qualities. Instead he impressed Harley as an animal of action and undoubtedly a seasoned leader.

Then there was the matter of his ears: Harley could not believe what they had just heard. Not only did these animals know Lucy, but more importantly they were going to her! Harley now realised he had also misjudged Lucy. She had put herself at risk, leaving home in order to help others. Harley felt a pang of guilt as he thought of his harsh attitude towards her.

Then, finally, there was the shock to his eyes. To his complete astonishment, he saw two fluffy rabbits happily hopping onto an alligator's armoured back, completely calmly and casually, as if it was the most ordinary thing in the world. Despite Harley's many experiences across the globe, nothing had stunned him like the sight he was seeing now.

Breaking free of his temporary, sensory-induced paralysis, Harley seized the moment. He reintroduced himself to the group, this time giving details that clarified who he was, his mission to rescue Lucy and how it had led him there. All the parties present listened attentively to his story, understanding what was said and what was left unsaid. Stripped away was the coat of pride, exposing a vulnerability and rawness Harley was not accustomed to allowing others to see.

Coming to the end of his tale, Harley began to feel self-conscious about such exposure, of them seeing the real dog behind the cloak. What if they found him lacking? Or, even worse, what if they didn't like him, especially as he now recognised that he had held some very wrong and prejudiced views about the very animals he was now asking to help him?

Instead, what one gator, a headstrong raccoon and two rabbits saw was a brave and loyal heart. They liked him instantly. Through their kindness and acceptance, Harley began to see the world in a different light, which helped him to become an even better version of his already pretty awesome self.

Then, in what would have been an unthinkable move for the old Harley, he trustingly boarded Big Dave's back, just as Bella and Michelle MacHare had done before him, followed by Phil Raccoon protecting the rear. With everyone safely aboard the friends pushed off from the bank (courtesy of Dave), leaving the familiarity of solid ground behind them. And so began their journey through the liquid blackness that is the swamp at night, steering them towards Lucy and Old Ashley Place.

After a very long and dark night's journey, the sun began to rise, illuminating and bringing shape to the world around them. In the distance the soft edges of the glade that was their destination began to come into view. Thanks to his companions, the journey had been both informative and pleasant for Harley. They talked about the marsh and ideas that might help to save it, and they shared some of their life stories. It was the sort of bond with others on a friendship level that Harley had not known existed. He was glad to now know otherwise. Though it was initially alien to him, Harley happily found he was adjusting quite well.

The conversation continued to flow effortlessly between him and his new friends, until Big Dave let out a happy squeal (equally as unexpected, coming from a large gator – and adorable too). Harley and his friends became just as excited when they saw what had merited such a squeal. There, up ahead on the edge of the glade, was Lucy. Harley felt relief, joy and a sense of accomplishment at the sight of her. Mostly, though, he was just glad to see her.

10
LUCY AND HARLEY HOST A POWWOW

As the sun began to rise over the marsh, Lucy decided to take a meditative stroll around the place she had once called home. She had, had a very busy past two days with her aunts and needed some time alone to think. Lucy paused at the edge of the glade where the swaying grass met the marsh's tea-coloured water. She had come expecting to find peace and serenity, hoping it would help to clear her mind.

Instead the sight before her caused her eyes to grow large in disbelief and her little cat mouth to involuntarily drop wide open with shock. Cutting through the early-morning fog and headed right for her was Harley, on top of her old friend Big Dave, accompanied by Phil Raccoon and the MacHare sisters. Of all the animals in the world she could possibly have encountered at this very moment, she never would have expected Harley to be one of them! Yet there he was, in her swamp with her old friends, and from the looks of things getting along quite brilliantly with them. And though she was more surprised than if she'd seen snow falling in the tropics, she was ever so glad to see him.

From the looks on their faces and the resounding whoop that Big Dave let out,

Lucy knew the feeling was mutual. The moment the friend flotilla reached land Lucy received her second shock of the morning. The very second Big Dave's back feet touched upon the grass, Harley joyfully jumped off his enormous scaled back and bounded over to Lucy, nearly knocking her over. He reminded her more of an excited puppy than the stiff, serious dog she had first met, and for the second time that morning she was glad to see him.

As soon as everyone got their bearings – their 'land legs', as Big Dave called it – Lucy led the group to Old Ashley Place. There they would join her aunts and begin brainstorming possible solutions to this awful situation. And though the reason for their presence was a sad one, Lucy knew that loyal friends were some of life's greatest gifts. This awareness filled her with gratitude and hope as they walked down the path to the old farmhouse.

Having heard voices, Fiona, Susan and Diana were all vigilantly waiting on the verandah; seeing the familiar faces, they collectively softened their stances and retracted their claws. The sisters surveyed the newly arrived party. All were known friends, with the exception of the large German shepherd.

'How curious,' Susan softly said under her breath.

'Indeed!' Fiona responded, and inquisitively stepped forward towards their mystery guest.

Seeing the perplexed look on her aunts' faces, Lucy began the introductions. When the warm greetings and explanations as to why they were all there were completed, the animals composed themselves into something of a circle and began discussing the possible actions that could be taken to save the marsh and their home. As the sun rose higher into the sky, the group came to the agreement that the task at hand was of such enormity that they would need input from all of the numerous groups that made up the diverse environment of the marsh. Only then could they know how all these different groups would be affected, what they wanted and what resources they had available.

Then Big Dave shared with the group a story, passed down from his great-grandfather, of an old tradition used by the native peoples that used to live as one with nature right there in the swamp.

When they needed to meet or make decisions of great importance, Big Dave said, the people would hold a special type of meeting. Everyone saw the wisdom in this tradition, and realised the necessity of conferring with others about the future of the marsh. So this is how—for the first time in over 150 years—the marsh was once again to host a Powwow.

The first thing to be done was to list all the major groups in the swamp and which members of them would make appropriate representatives. Not that all voices weren't valuable, but some were more suited to the task at hand. For example, Jerry Bullfrog was a lovely fellow but he happened to have a very hard time sitting still for more than two seconds at a time; he also had a penchant for licking everything and everyone in sight, just in case he could pick up a tasty fly, then hopping away with a laugh reminiscent of the Mad Hatter's.

Once this long and exhaustive list was created and then agreed upon, the next step was to decide how to most efficiently and effectively get the invitations out to the participants, and how to safely transport them to Old Ashley Place for the Powwow. Being that this step of the process required a lot of creative, out-of-the-box thinking, discussions took them late into the afternoon. While careful and detailed planning is often key to a plan's success, time was not on the friends' side. Several of the representatives were diurnal creatures, meaning that they were only awake during daytime hours. The group had to hurry.

Since the friends didn't know how much time they had to come up with a solution or, in the very worst case, an evacuation and rehousing plan, it was decided that the Powwow was to be held at sunrise the very next day. Thankfully Nico, Wendy, Owen and Evan had all stayed on after helping Lucy get to her aunts. With their assistance the group was able to recruit several other fish and birds to help get the message out across the marsh.

By midnight all the invitations had been delivered. The marsh was now buzzing with nervous energy. This was the first time that most of the marsh residents were hearing about the possible destruction of their homes. While fear and anger were the emotions communally felt, the residents were also very grateful that a group had formed and taken the initiative to help save the marsh, and protect their lives and homes. In hosting the Powwow, Lucy and her friends had given the marsh residents a feeling far more important and powerful than fear or anger. They had given them hope.

Every invitation was accepted. That night, nocturnal or not, every creature was awake, and the usually still marsh came alive with hurried movement as the Powwow attendees made their way to Old Ashley Place. Animals who normally avoided each other or didn't get along, whether through a personality clash or a predator–prey relationship, put their differences aside and united under their shared hope and goal, and worked together to make sure all the attending representatives were able to safely get to the Powwow.

By dawn's first light, each of the representatives had arrived and were gathered together. Seeing that they were all ready and empowered to save their homes, Lucy prepared to call for the Powwow to come to order.

Then the ground began to shake, and a deep, terrible rumble was felt by all.

The loud, incessant noise seemed to reverberate off every living thing and structure that surrounded them. Their eyes widened in panic and their hearts filled with terror when they saw what was causing the disturbance.

11
MAMIE LACEY COMES UP
WITH A PLAN

After the town meeting had come to its disappointing end, Mamie Lacey had launched herself into researching state laws that might help her put a stop to ConMan's development plans. It was while doing some digging in the records held in the town's courthouse that she came across a folder of old land deeds. Among them was the original deed for Old Ashley Place, purchased in 1881 by a Mr Richard Brush. Feeling a flutter of hope and excitement, Mamie Lacey asked the county clerk if there were more documents to go along with the purchase of that land. When the very sweet blue-haired county clerk returned, she brought with her a large stack of paperwork that contained maps outlining the boundaries of the purchase, numerous photographs of the land within those boundaries and the property's financial history.

Mamie Lacey learned that Mr Brush had never sold the land; technically it was still owned private property. However, quite a lot of back taxes had accumulated, since no one had been paying taxes on the property for over a century. After explaining this to Mamie, the county clerk conspiratorially lowered her voice and informed Mamie that anyone who came along and paid those back taxes could own the land, even if they didn't have the deed.

It was at this moment that Mamie Lacey came up with a plan.

With the figure of the total amount owed in her hand, Mamie Lacey called Greg Lacey to discuss her idea, and then ran all the way to her bank. By close of business that day Mamie and Greg Lacey were the proud owners of Old Ashley Place and the 650 acres that surrounded it.

As soon as the Laceys were given their officiated temporary deed, they headed over to the ConMan office. Unfortunately it had already closed for the day so the office was empty. Frustrated, Mamie peered through the window, hoping to find someone who might have stayed late at work. Scanning the room for signs of movement, Mamie Lacey's eyes came across a large bulletin board with the words 'Launch at Dawn' written across it. She got a sinking feeling in the pit of her stomach. Pulling out her mobile phone, Mamie Lacey first called the town mayor, then the chief of police, then anyone and everyone she thought might be able to help.

Two hours before dawn, alarms began to chime in the Lacey household. Mamie and Greg Lacey, who hadn't really slept due to nervous anticipation, jumped out of bed, quickly getting ready to head down to Old Ashley Place and fight for what was now rightly theirs. Due to the heavy rains that spring, all roads leading into the marsh were still flooded. So they headed to the town marina, where the mayor, the chief of police and two additional police officers waited in the police boat. Several of their friends were there too, waiting to help. There were even those who showed up on their jetskis to lend additional support and a show of strength. But in all the excitement they had forgotten about Harley.

As soon as everyone was ready, the boats cast off, navigating across the harbour and towards Old Ashley Place. The 'Save the Marsh' team, as they now referred to themselves, were on their way. Help was coming and not a moment too soon.

12
TIME RUNS OUT

For a brief moment that felt like an eternity, the Powwow attendees collectively froze in horror as their minds processed what their eyes were seeing. A frightening procession of large machines, armed with dangerous-looking tools solely designed for destruction, had begun rolling off a heavy steel cargo ship and towards Old Ashley Place. It appeared that the marsh residents had run out of time. If they were going to save their home they would have to act now.

Harley was the first to unfreeze and take action. Having already experienced threatening and hostile situations, his military instincts and training kicked in. He knew that any possibility of success depended not only on keeping himself calm and clear-headed but on doing the same for the entire group. He surveyed the group and their surroundings, evaluating their strengths and any possible element that could give them an advantage. He knew fighting destruction with destruction was a pointless battle approach. These machines were far too strong and powerful to try to attack; that would only lead to certain doom.

Then it dawned on him: what had

brought every single one of them to the Powwow? Hope, and love. This was their strength. These most powerful of convictions would be their defence.

In a composed and confident voice, Harley briefed the group on his plan. Lucy listened to his strategy with both pride and admiration. Here was this brave dog she had only known for a few days, valiantly putting himself in danger to help save her and the marshland. Lucy was moved with gratitude.

Working together, Harley and Lucy began organising the marsh residents to make their big stand against the advancing demolition machines. Time had run out for our friends, and the moment for action had come. Swallowing their fear and nervousness, the marsh residents courageously assembled as instructed, and prepared to face down their enemy and save their home. They had one shot and they were going to make it count.

13
AN UNEXPECTED SIGHT

Racing across the harbour, the Save the Marsh team soon had Old Ashley Place in their sights, and a few minutes later arrived at their destination. Tying off their boats and other vessels to the rickety old dock, they ignored any concern they might have normally felt about the aging structure's poor condition and jumped out of their boats, running as quickly as possible along the dock towards the demolition machines they could hear rumbling ahead.

As the team breathlessly closed the gap between them and the demolition crew, what they saw just ahead of the machines caused them to stop in their tracks.

Exactly what the team saw is still very much argued about to this day. Before their eyes, bravely joined together in unity and love, stood every type of marsh animal conceivable, holding paws, claws, wings, hoofs, legs and even fins in a line of defiance and strength. Alligators, rabbits, birds of every sort, raccoons, possums and even snakes all formed a continuous chain of resistance. And right in the middle of it all stood Lucy and Harley, Mamie and Greg Lacey's very own missing cat and dog.

This unexpected sight was as shocking

as it was moving, and its profound message was missed by no one present – including the demolition machine operators, who shifted their gears into neutral and brought the machines to a halt. Seizing the opportunity created by the stand-off, Mamie Lacey, with deed in hand and rights to the land, proceeded to kick ConMan and its machines off her land.

News of what happened at Old Ashley Place quickly spread around town and beyond, eventually finding its place among other popular town legends. For some the story was a sweet fable with fairytale elements; others thought that, due to lack of sleep and the tricks early morning light can play on the eyes, it was something like a desert mirage. Yet there are still others who believe. In all the years that have passed not one person who was at Old Ashley Place that day ever changed their story or lost that very rare and special childlike sparkle of amazement and wonder in their smile when they recounted the events of that day.

I am of the personal belief that the non-believers just don't know the full story of Harley and Lucy, the story that you and I know. Whether or not you choose to believe it is completely up to you. I know I do, and my world is a more magical and special place for it. However, either way, what is important is that on that day individuals with hope and determination came together and, in their unity, found the strength to make a stand, thus saving the marshland and all who call that unique and beautiful place home.

In time, Mamie and Greg Lacey were able to clear up the administrative nightmare ConMan had created in their almost successful attempt to destroy and build on the marsh. Once this process was finally completed, the Laceys decided it would be better to be proactive rather than reactive, so they turned the property and all its land into a wildlife refuge and nature reserve. In this way they protected the marsh and all those who called it home from any future threat of destruction.

Lucy and Harley could not have been prouder of their humans. They became the best of friends, sharing many more hair-raising, action-packed adventures together.

But those are stories for another time.

REFLECTION QUESTIONS

1. a) In life, all things change. When one chapter comes to an end, a new one begins. How do you feel about change? b) What are some things we can do to help us deal with change in a positive way?

2. Dogs really can serve in and retire from the military services. What are some other occupations that animals work in?

3. a) When Lucy meets Harley for the first time, she greets him in a way he is unfamiliar with, resulting in a misunderstanding. Around the world, people of different cultures have unique greeting traditions. Can you name a few? b) If an argument did occur when you first met someone new, how could you

fix the situation?

4. In the story, animals as well as humans hold community meetings. Why is a sense of community important?

5. How do you feel about buildings being put on undeveloped land?

6. What features and creatures make up the unique marshland habitat in the story?

7. Why is it so important to protect our environment?

8. What are some things you can do yourself to help make a positive impact on both the environment and your community?

9. Mamie Lacey, Lucy and Harley all face challenges throughout the book; however, each of them is able to overcome obstacles in their own way.

What are some challenges you have faced and how have you handled them?

ABOUT THE AUTHOR

Maria Atlan, a former Military Officer, is a writer of poetry, short stories, and all things conservation related - from academic articles to children's literature. She is a lover of travel and adventure, both of which have served to strengthen her desire to protect our planet and share that need with others.

When she is not abroad working with conservation projects, Maria can be found at home in Fort Lauderdale, Florida, with her much beloved menagerie of animals.

ABOUT THE ILLUSTRATOR

Adriana Santos lives in Seville, Spain, where she was born and studied Fine Arts at university. After working for almost twelve years as a graphic designer, she followed her childhood dream and her work is now focused on children's picture books and middle grade illustration. She loves filling her work with playfulness, hidden details, vibrant colours and tenderness. She usually likes to mix working in pencils and pen with the bright and intense colours of digital work.

In her free time, she reads books and hangs out with her children: two big sources of inspiration for her work.